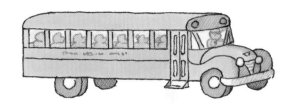

The Berenstain Bears
Go Back to School

The Berenstain Bears
Go Back to School

Stan & Jan Berenstain
with Mike Berenstain

HarperCollins*Publishers*

Library of Congress Cataloging-in-Publication Data
Berenstain, Stan, 1923–
   The Berenstain Bears go back to school / Stan and Jan Berenstain ; with [illustrations by] Mike Berenstain.— 1st ed.
      p. cm. — (Berenstain Bears)
   Summary: On the first day of the new school year, the Berenstain cubs are reminded that "though school is a challenge, it can also be fun."
   ISBN 0-06-052673-4 — ISBN 0-06-052674-2 (lib. bdg.)
   [1. First day of school—Fiction. 2. Schools—Fiction. 3. Bears—Fiction. 4. Stories in rhyme.] I. Berenstain, Jan, 1923– II. Berenstain, Michael, ill. III. Title.
PZ8.3.B4493Bhdhe 2005
   [E]—dc22
                                                                                                      2004004339

Typography by Matt Adamec 6 7 8 9 10 ❖ First Edition

When summer ends
and the air turns cool,
the time has come
to go back to school.

Sister and Brother Bear,
all clean and neat,
wait at the bus stop
just up the street.

Cousin Fred and Lizzy
are waiting there, too,
with some kindergartners—
for them this is new!

When down the road
comes the big orange bus!
And there at the wheel
is bus driver Gus!

The bus slows down;
its lights flash red.
Now Brother and Sister
and Lizzy and Fred
all climb aboard.
They're on their way
to Bear Country School
on this special first day.

As they pass their house,
cubs Sister and Brother
smile and wave
to their father and mother.

Country School

Down the sunny dirt road
waiting just up ahead
is Bear Country School,
newly painted bright red.

The classrooms are waiting
for the day to begin,
all dusted and polished
and neat as a pin.

The whiteboards are waiting
for the whine and screech
of markers wielded by teachers
with lessons to teach.

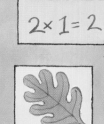

$$2 \times 1 = 2$$

It's the first day of school
for all teachers, too.
One of the teachers
is brand-spanking new.
Ms. Polly's her name.
She tries to stay cool
even though it is also
her first day of school.

And now here they come!
Right up Schoolhouse Drive!
The big orange buses
are about to arrive!

Now off the buses
the cubs come a-pouring!
Torrents of students
all cheering and roaring!

The schoolyard was empty
the whole summer long,
but now it's alive
with a noisy cub throng.

Cubs playing tag.
Cubs jumping rope.
Kindergartners doing
their very best to cope.

Yikes! The Too-Tall Gang
is headed this way
to tease all the cubs
who are smaller than they.

Here comes Mr. Grizzmeyer,
who coaches sports.
"Report to my office,"
Mr. Grizzmeyer snorts.

The sound of the bell
cuts through all the noise
of a whole schoolyard teeming
with cub girls and boys.

Cubs get into line
according to size,
checking out new backpacks
and cool school supplies.

Nothing has changed
as they march through the halls.
The very same pictures
still hang on the walls.

The principal's bench
where naughty cubs wait,
sitting so quietly
awaiting their fate.

The sports trophy case,
all filled with prizes,
gold cups and ribbons
of various sizes.

There's Teacher Jane
greeting her new class,
welcoming every
cub lad and lass.

And all out of breath
from one last game of tag,
all cubs pledge allegiance
to our country's flag.

Then as she writes
the lesson of the day,
a stray paper airplane
flies teacher's way.

"You know I've got eyes
in the back of my head,"
says Teacher Jane
to naughty cub Ned.

And it's just possible
that she maybe had.
She does always know
just who's being bad.

Meanwhile, in grade three,
just up the way,
Teacher Bob
starts out this way,

"Third grade is hard.
Third grade is tough.
There's no more easy
First-gradish stuff.

antidisestablishmentarianism

"There'll be geography
and math and science,
book reports, history,
and self-reliance,
vocabulary words
as long as your arm."
The third graders listen
with growing alarm.
"Gulp!" says Brother Bear.
"Groan!" says Freddy,
both wondering whether
they are really quite ready.

The recess bell rings!
Hooray! Hooray!
Out go the cubs
to run and to play.
Hopscotch! Dodgeball!
King of the hill!
"How about *queen*?"
proposes cub Jill.

"I'll tell you what,"
says Sister to Lizzy.
"Let's wind up the swings
and let's get all dizzy."

The bell rings again!
There's work to be done!
Though school is a challenge,
it can also be fun.

Before long comes the ring
of the closing bell.
Both cubs and teachers
have done pretty well.

Cubs hop on the bus
at the end of the day,
heading for home.
The bus knows the way.

To the tree house where Mama
and Papa are waiting.
Off the bus come the cubs,
noisily celebrating.

Bear Country School

Says Brother, "We made
a pretty good start."
"Look," says Sister,
"I did this in art."

"How lovely!" says Mama.
"It's our home sweet tree."
After supper, some homework
and a bit of TV.

The cubs lie awake
in their double-deck bed.
Both are thinking about
all the fun days ahead.

There is so much to do.
There is so much to know.
There are so many ways
to learn and to grow.

So they lie awake thinking
That first school-day night
about places to go,
about stories to write,
about saving the forests,
about cleaning the air,
about getting along
with their fellow bear.

They could dig up old bones,
discover new creatures,
save the whale and the condor.
Hey! Maybe be teachers!

Miss Sister Bear

Whales

But before very long
now they are dozing.
Brother's and Sister's
eyes are now closing.

And so to sleep.
"Sleep tight" is the rule.
There's a big day tomorrow—
the second day of school!

For Tony, with love
_MCB

For Ella + Alan
_TM

This edition published by Scholastic Inc., 557 Broadway; New York, NY 10012,
by arrangement with Little Tiger Press.
SCHOLASTIC and associated logos are trademarks and/or registered
trademarks of Scholastic Inc.
Scholastic Canada; Markham, Ontario

First published in the United States by Good Books
Library of Congress Cataloging-in-Publication Data
is available for this title.

Original edition published in English by Little Tiger Press,
an imprint of Magi Publications, London, England, 2004.

Text copyright © M. Christina Butler 2004
Illustrations copyright © Tina Macnaughton 2004

ISBN 13: 978-1-84506-602-4
ISBN 10: 1-84506-602-2

Printed in China

One Snowy Night

M. Christina Butler

Pictures by Tina Macnaughton

The cold wind woke Little Hedgehog
from his deep winter sleep. It blew his
blanket of leaves high into the air,
and he shivered in the snow. He tried
to sleep again, but he was much too cold.

Suddenly, something fell from the sky . . .

...THUD!

It landed right in front of his nose.
It was a present, and it had his name on it.

To Little Hedgehog
With Love From
Father Christmas xx

Little Hedgehog opened
the present as fast as he
could. Inside was a red
wooly hat . . .
hedgehog size!

He put it on at once.
He pulled it to the back.
He pulled it to the front.
He pulled it to one side,
then the other . . .

But it didn't matter how he stretched it
to fit. His prickles got in the way *every time*.
By now the hat was much too big for a
little hedgehog.

He took it off and stared at it,
until at last he had an idea . . .

He gave the hat a shake
and wrapped it up again.
He ripped a piece off the
label and wrote on
the rest.

Then he ran to Rabbit's house.
Rabbit was out, so he left the present
on his doorstep.

It was snowing hard as
Little Hedgehog tried to find his
way back home. The snowflakes flew
all around, and he wasn't sure
which way to go.

"Oh dear, oh dear," he said as he
wandered around. "I shouldn't have
come out in this weather. But I know
Rabbit will be happy to have a nice
wooly hat to wear."

"Too much snow!" said Rabbit, rushing home. He saw the present lying on his doorstep.

"What's this?" he squeaked with delight, ripping off the paper. "A wooly hat," he cried. "For ME!"

Happy Christmas Rabbit
With Love from
Little Hedgehog xx

He put it on at once. He tried it with
his ears inside, and then outside.
He pulled it this way and
he pulled it that way.
But it didn't matter how
he stretched it to fit.
His ears got in
the way . . .
every time.

By now the hat was
much much bigger. It was
much too big for a rabbit.
So . . .

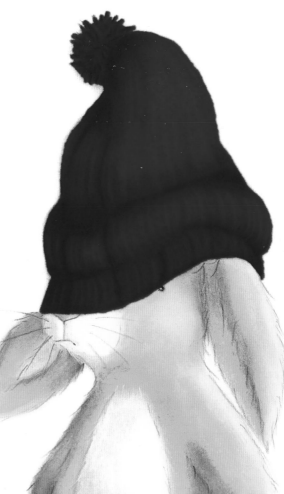

. . . Rabbit wrapped up the hat
and wrote on a corner of the label.
Then he went to visit Badger.

The cold weather made Badger
very grumpy.
  "Merry Christmas, Badger!"
shouted Rabbit.
  "Who's there?" growled Badger.
  "Merry Christmas!" repeated Rabbit,
giving him the present.

"A Christmas present?"
asked Badger.
"For ME?"

Badger put the hat on.
He pulled it down over his ears.
  "How . . . about . . . THAT!"
he said, looking in the mirror.
  "Very nice," said Rabbit.
  "What did you say?" said Badger.
  "Very nice!" yelled Rabbit,
hopping off.

"Don't you like it?" asked
Badger, turning around.
But Rabbit had gone.
   Badger took the hat off.
"I can't use this hat,"
he said. "I can't hear
a thing. Too bad—it's such
a nice color."

So Badger wrapped up
the present and marched
off to Fox's house.
He didn't use
a label.

Fox was going out exploring.

"Here you are, friend," said Badger merrily.

"A Christmas present, just for you!"

"Christmas?" snapped Fox, puzzled.

"Yes, Christmas!" called Badger.

"Time to be nice to each other!"

And he trudged home.

"A hat?" sneered Fox, opening the present. "Why would I want a hat?"
    Then he looked at the hat again . . .

He made two holes for his ears and put it on. Satisfied, he went on his way.

The white fields twinkled in the moonlight. Fox sniffed around and found a small trail. He followed it this way and that way until suddenly it stopped. There was something under the snow!

Fox dug and dug,
until he found a small hedgehog.
It was cold and did not move.
 "Poor little guy," said Fox.
He put the hedgehog inside the
red wooly hat and carried
it to Rabbit's house.

Rabbit and Badger were having supper.
"Look what I've found in the snow!"
cried Fox, bursting in.
They all looked into
the hat.

"A hedgehog?" asked Badger.
"What's a hedgehog doing out at
Christmas time? He should be fast asleep!"
  "It's my friend Little Hedgehog!" cried
Rabbit. "He must have gotten lost going
home in the snow!"
  Little Hedgehog opened his eyes.
"Hello," he said sleepily. "Oh, this
is such a lovely warm blanket."

The friends all looked at each other.
Rabbit grinned and Fox scratched his head.
  "Hmmm," said Badger. "I think this wooly
hat is *just right* for Little Hedgehog!"
  "Merry Christmas, Little Hedgehog!"
they all cheered . . . but Little Hedgehog
was fast asleep.

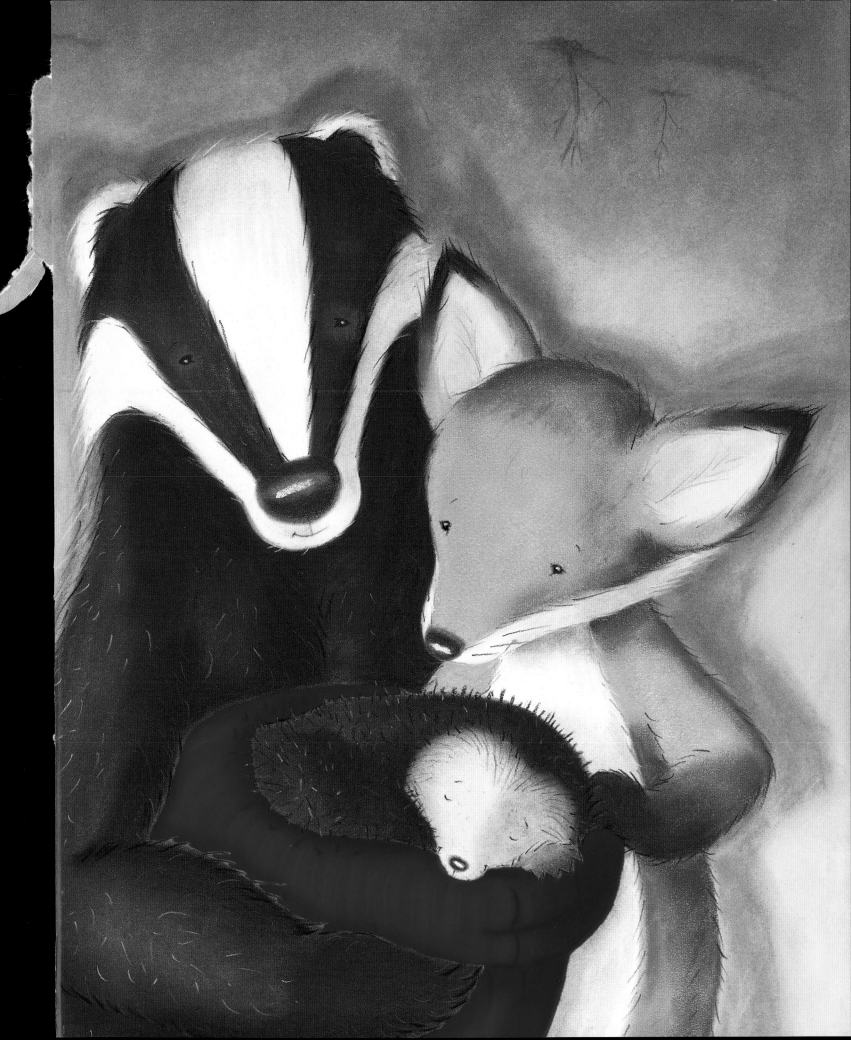